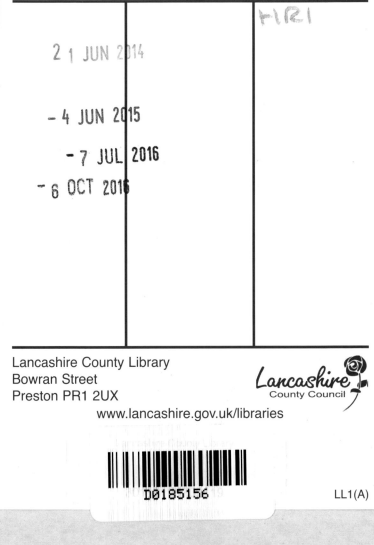

First published in Great Britain by HarperCollins *Children's Books* in 2014
HarperCollins *Children's Books* is a division of HarperCollins*Publishers* Ltd,
77-85 Fulham Palace Road, Hammersmith, London, W6 8JB.

The HarperCollins website address is: www.harpercollins.co.uk

1

Text © Hothouse Fiction Limited 2014
Illustrations © HarperCollins *Children's Books*, 2014
Illustrations by Dynamo

ISBN 978-0-00-755007-4

Printed and bound in England by Clays Ltd, St Ives plc

CHRIS BLAKE

TIME HUNTERS

COWBOY SHOWDOWN

HarperCollins *Children's Books*

Travel through time with Tom

adventures!

Gladiator Clash

Knight Quest

Viking Raiders

Greek Warriors

Pirate Mutiny

Egyptian Curse

Cowboy Showdown

Samurai Assassin

Outback Outlaw

Stone Age Rampage

Mohican Brave

Aztec Attack

For games, competitions and more visit:

www.time-hunters.com

CONTENTS

With special thanks to Lisa Fiedler

PROLOGUE

1500 AD, Mexico

As far as Zuma was concerned, there were only two good things about being a human sacrifice. One was the lovely black pendant the tribal elders had given her to wear. The other was the little Chihuahua dog the high priest had just placed next to her.

I've always wanted a pet, thought Zuma, as the trembling pup cuddled beside her. *Though this does seem like an extreme way to get one.*

Zuma lay on an altar at the top of the Great Pyramid. In honour of the mighty Aztec rain god, Tlaloc, she'd been painted bright blue and wore a feathered headdress.

The entire village had turned out to watch the slave girl be sacrificed in exchange for plentiful rainfall and a good harvest. She could see her master strutting in the crowd below, proud to have supplied the slave for today's sacrifice. He looked a little relieved too. And Zuma couldn't blame him. As slaves went, she was a troublesome one, always trying to run away. But she couldn't help it – her greatest dream was to be free!

Zuma had spent the entire ten years of her life in slavery, and she was sick of it. She knew she should be honoured to be a sacrifice, but she had a much better plan – to escape!

"Besides," she said, frowning at her painted skin, "blue is not my colour!"

"Hush, slave!" said the high priest, Acalan, his face hidden by a jade mask. "The ceremony is about to begin." He raised his knife in the air.

"Shame I'll be missing it," said Zuma. "Tell Tlaloc I'd like to take a *rain* check." As the priest lowered the knife, she pulled up her

knees and kicked him hard in the stomach
with both feet.

"*Oof!*" The priest doubled over, clutching
his belly. The blade clattered to the floor.

Zuma rolled off the altar, dodging the
other priests, who fell over each other in their
attempts to catch her. One priest jumped into
her path, but the little Chihuahua dog sank
his teeth into the man's ankle. As the priest
howled in pain, Zuma whistled to the dog.

"Nice work, doggie!" she said. "I'm

getting out of here and you're coming with me!" She scooped him up and dashed down the steps of the pyramid.

"Grab her!" groaned the high priest from above.

Many hands reached out to catch the slave girl, but Zuma was fast and determined. She bolted towards the jungle bordering the pyramid. Charging into the cool green leaves, she ran until she could no longer hear the shouts of the crowd.

"We did it," she said to the dog. "We're free!"

As she spoke, the sky erupted in a loud rumble of thunder, making the dog yelp. "Thunder's nothing to be scared of," said Zuma.

"Don't be so sure about that!" came a deep voice above her.

Zuma looked up to see a creature with blue skin and long, sharp fangs, like a jaguar. He carried a wooden drum and wore a feathered headdress, just like Zuma's.

She knew at once who it was. "Tlaloc!" she gasped.

The rain god's bulging eyes glared down at her. "You have dishonoured me!" he bellowed. "No sacrifice has ever escaped before!"

"Really? I'm the first?" Zuma beamed

with pride, but the feeling didn't last long. Tlaloc's scowl was too scary.

"I'm sorry!" she said quietly. "I just wanted to be free."

"You will *never* be free!" Tlaloc hissed. "Unless you can escape again…"

Tlaloc banged his drum, and thunder rolled through the jungle.

He pounded the drum a second time, and thick black clouds gathered high above the treetops.

"This isn't looking good," Zuma whispered. Holding the dog tight, she closed her eyes.

On the third deafening drum roll, the jungle floor began to shake and a powerful force tugged at Zuma. She felt her whole body being swallowed up inside… the drum!

CHAPTER 1
DRUM ROLL, PLEASE

Tom Sullivan hurried ahead of his dad. He was never able to just walk through the museum where his dad worked. Tom was a history fanatic and he loved being at the museum – there was always so much to see!

"C'mon, Dad," he urged. "I want to look at the 'Treasures of the Aztec World' exhibition before it opens next week."

"It's not quite finished yet," Dad

warned. "There are still lots of artefacts in shipping crates."

"I don't mind," said Tom. "I can help you unpack."

Tom loved helping his dad at the museum, especially when it was closed to the public. Then he could make as much noise as he wanted, and study the displays without the crowds.

As they reached the Egyptian hall, Tom felt a rush of excitement. Not long ago, in this very place, he'd accidentally broken an ancient statue and freed the princess Isis from a curse. Together, they had travelled through time to find the six lost amulets Isis needed to enter the Afterlife. They'd met pirates and Vikings and Roman gladiators. But even though they'd faced fearsome opponents, Tom and Isis had managed to collect all six jewels.

It had been the most amazing experience of Tom's life.

Weeks had passed since he and Isis had had their last adventure, and life was much quieter now. Actually, Tom was surprised to find it was a little *too* quiet.

Finally, they reached the Aztec room. As soon as they entered the hall, Tom gasped. He felt as though he'd just stepped back in time to Ancient Mexico. There were still several unpacked crates and boxes, but the things that had been unloaded were amazing.

"The Aztecs created a truly great empire," his father explained. "It reached its peak around 1500 AD. But in my opinion, their most brilliant contribution was discovering something we could not live without."

"What's that?" asked Tom.

"Chocolate!"

"Chocolate?" Tom laughed. "Well, I guess we really owe them then!" He pointed to a model of a twin pyramid with a squared-off top. "What's this?"

"That's the Great Temple in Tenochtitlan," said Dad. "It was dedicated to the gods Tlaloc and Huitzilopochtli."

"Hoo-zee *whats*y?"

Before Dad could reply, a woman appeared in the doorway. "Dr Sullivan, there's a call for you," she said.

"I'll be right back," said Dad, heading to his office. "Take a look round, but be careful and *don't* touch anything."

Tom studied the displays. He saw clay statues with wide mouths and big ears, sword-like weapons and documents written in a strange language. There was even a carved wooden box that looked like a treasure chest.

In a corner he found a wooden cylinder carved with strange symbols. The label explained it was a drum that belonged to the rain god, Tlaloc, who would bang it to create thunder! Beside it lay two mallets.

This I've got to hear! thought Tom. He reached for one of the mallets, then quickly drew back his hand. Tom knew the rules, but his fingers were itching. It was as if the drum were begging him to play it. He knew he shouldn't, but he was just too curious.

Tom glanced round to be sure there was nobody else in the room. Then he picked up a mallet and gently swung it down.

To his shock, an enormous roll of thunder exploded from the drum. Aztec objects shook on their shelves as the sound echoed through the room.

Suddenly, Tom wasn't alone any more.

Standing in front of him was a girl about his age. At least he *thought* she was a girl. But he'd never seen a blue girl wearing a feathered headdress before.

"You freed me from that drum!" the girl exclaimed, throwing her arms round Tom. "Thank you!"

Tom stepped back and nearly tripped over something scampering beneath his feet. A little dog was wildly wagging its tail and nipping at Tom's trainers.

"Don't mind him," said the girl. "He's just showing you how grateful he is. He was trapped in the drum too."

"I didn't *mean* to do anything," said Tom, reaching down to pat the tiny dog.

The girl frowned as she looked round the Aztec hall. "Some of these things look familiar," she said, pointing to a shelf full of pottery. "But you don't." She narrowed her eyes. "Are you my new master?"

"Your new *what*?"

The next thing Tom knew, the girl

was shifting from foot to foot like a boxer – elbows cocked, hands curled into fists.

"Well, you can forget it," she said. "I'll never be a slave again. I'll fight you for my freedom if I have to!"

Tom had no intention of fighting with this feathery blue stranger. "I'm *not* your master! I just banged the drum and the next thing I knew, you appeared."

"Oh." The girl dropped her fists and grinned. "Then I'm very glad you got me out of there. My name's Zuma. I'm an Aztec slave. Or at least, I used to be."

Once again, the museum was rocked by an ear-splitting thunderclap. But this time Tom and the drum had nothing to do with it. The little dog yelped and jumped into Zuma's arms. Heavy rain began to fall… *inside* the museum!

Maybe something set off the sprinkler system? Tom thought. But since when did the sprinkler system include thunder? Something very strange was going on.

"Help me cover the artefacts," Tom shouted. "We have to protect them!"

"You *sound* like a master," Zuma grumbled. She put down the dog and dashed about after Tom, putting the ancient objects in glass display cases.

They only managed to rescue a few items before another rumble of thunder shook the room. A second stranger appeared before Tom. This one had blue skin and fancy feathers. Only *he* was enormous!

Zuma and the dog looked nervous. Tom could only stare.

"Please tell me this is your much larger,

but extremely *friendly*, twin brother," Tom whispered.

Zuma shook her head. "He's Tlaloc, the rain god," she whispered. "I was supposed to be sacrificed to him, but I escaped." She rolled her eyes. "I can't believe he's still angry about that."

"Take it from me," Tom muttered, thinking of the Egyptian god Anubis. "These gods like to hold a grudge."

Tlaloc picked up the wooden drum and the rain stopped.

"Zuma! You have escaped your prison after five hundred years!" Tlaloc roared. The clay bowls clattered on their glass shelves. "But you arc not free yet!"

The rain god pointed one huge finger at the treasure chest. The lid lifted with a loud creak. Even though he was scared, Tom was

impressed by the god's magic. The chest was filled with gold coins, each bearing the image of an Aztec sun. Tlaloc waved his hand and six shiny coins rose out of the chest and sailed across the room. They landed with a jangle in his palm.

"You must find these six sun coins in order to earn your freedom," Tlaloc announced. "When you have collected all six, you can return to your time as a free person."

The god banged the drum and thunder rumbled. He waved his hand and a powerful wind gusted through the room, bringing with it a thick, white mist. Tlaloc tossed the coins into the mist. For a moment they spun, shining in the air. Then the wind howled again and they vanished.

"What's happening?" Zuma cried, her feathered headdress flapping wildly.

Tom was pretty sure he knew what was coming next. Heart pounding, he reached down and scooped up the little dog as the mist surrounded them. "Grab my hand," he shouted, "and hold on tight!"

"Where are we going?" Zuma cried.

The edges of the museum began to fade as the mist swirled into a whirlwind. "I'm not sure where... or when... we'll land," Tom shouted above the howl of the cyclone. "But one thing I do know – it's going to be an adventure!"

CHAPTER 2
MIRROR, MIRROR

Tom and Zuma tumbled out of the cyclone and found themselves in the middle of a wood. Green pine trees towered above them. Here and there, beams of sunlight trickled through the branches.

Zuma scrambled to her feet. "Did that really happen?" Her voice was filled with panic.

"It certainly did," Tom said. He hardly recognised Zuma. She was no longer covered

in blue paint and feathers, and the only thing
that remained of her Aztec costume was the
black, mirror-like pendant that hung round
her neck. Zuma's long hair was almost as
black and shiny as the mirror, and her skin
was the colour of caramel. Right now, her
dark brown eyes were darting nervously
about the woods.

"Where are we?" she asked.

"I don't know," said Tom. "But I'm pretty sure we aren't in England any more."

Zuma tilted her head, confused. "Where's England?"

"That's where I live," said Tom. "Thousands of miles from Mexico, where you live. I mean, lived."

The little dog scurried over and pawed at Zuma's feet until she picked him up.

"He's got a lot of energy for such a little thing," Tom remarked. "What's he called?"

"I don't know," said Zuma. "We've only just met. He was going to be sacrificed, like me. I saved him."

"You should give him a name," said Tom, and the dog let out a woof of agreement.

Zuma laughed. "OK. Well, let's see… he's pretty lively. Maybe we should call him

after something that has a lot of zing. Like…
Chilli!"

"Perfect!" said Tom.

The dog wagged his tail and licked
Zuma's cheek. He seemed to like his new
name.

"It's as if he understands," said Zuma.

"Speaking of understanding… the two of
us speak different languages, so we shouldn't
be able to understand each other, but we do.
If it's like the last time I went time travelling,
we'll understand everyone we meet too."

"But how's that possible?" asked Zuma.

Tom shrugged. "It must be part of Tlaloc's
magic."

Now Zuma noticed Tom's clothing
and giggled. "What *are* you wearing?" She
looked down at her own outfit. "What am *I*
wearing?"

"They're dungarees," said Tom, brushing off the knees of his sturdy denim trousers. "And I think these checked shirts are made of cotton."

"What about these strange sandals?" Zuma lifted one foot, then the other.

"Not sandals…" Tom corrected her with a grin. "Boots. *Cowboy* boots!" He reached up and tipped the hat on his head. "And cowboy hats."

Zuma looked up at the wide brim on her own hat. "Well, it beats feathers!"

Now Chilli began pawing the dirt at Zuma's feet.

"Good idea, Chilli," said Zuma. "Let's start looking for that first coin. The sooner we find it, the sooner I can be free!" While Chilli dug, Zuma began searching under rocks and round tree roots.

"You're not going to find it like that," said Tom. "We need a clue."

"Where do we get one of those?" said Zuma.

Tom frowned and thought back to his adventures with Isis. She'd had a scarab ring that had given them help in the form of riddles…

Tom looked Zuma up and down. His eyes stopped on her necklace. "Your pendant!"

Zuma touched the black disc. "The high priest made me wear it for the sacrifice because black mirrors are good for communicating with spirits and predicting the future."

"Perfect!" cried Tom. "Ask it for help."

Zuma held the pendant with both hands. "Er… what should I say?"

"Well, you can always be like Snow

White and start with, 'Mirror, Mirror…'"
Tom burst out laughing when he saw the
strange look Zuma was giving him. "Oh,
right. I guess you didn't have fairy tales in
Aztec times." Tom quickly explained how
Snow White had summoned the voice of her
magic mirror.

"OK, here goes," said Zuma.

"Mirror, Mirror, on a chain,
Can you help us? Please explain!
We are lost and must be told
How to find the coins of gold."

Tom smiled. "Nice."
The next instant, silvery sparks appeared
on the smooth surface of the mirror, followed
by words rising up from the dark stone:

In a town that has no law,
The hero must always be first to draw;
Where rivers and coaches rush with gold
Fortunes are won but souls can be sold.
The sharpest of shooters you'll meet on this trip;
One is a marshal who's smart as a whip.
The West can be wild, it's not for the meek,
So be brave in the cave when you roll out of
Spring Creek!

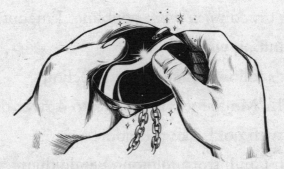

"Now I know where we are," cried Tom.
"We've landed in the Wild West."

"Hmm," said Zuma, looking worried.

"Exactly how wild is it?"

"I'm not sure," Tom admitted. "All I know is that in the late 1800s, gold was discovered in America's West. Thousands of people hurried there to try and get rich. That's why they called it the Gold Rush—"

"Babbling!" Zuma cupped her hand to her ear. "I hear babbling."

Tom looked hurt. "Well you did *ask*…"

"No," said Zuma, patting his shoulder. "I didn't mean *you* were babbling. I meant I hear running water."

"Let's follow it," said Tom, feeling hopeful. "Maybe it will lead us to a river that rushes with gold, like the riddle says."

With Chilli trotting along beside them, Tom and Zuma found their way to a creek. Then they followed its winding bank through the trees and scrub.

The further they walked, the more the woods thinned. Soon they arrived at the edge of a clearing, where the creek broadened into a wide pool. Standing knee-deep in the rippling water were two boys. The taller one looked like he was in his late teens while the smaller boy was only a bit older than Tom and Zuma.

"What are they doing?" Tom whispered.

"I think they're searching for gold," Zuma explained. They watched the boys dunk shallow pans into the water. Every so often, one of them would let out a joyful 'Woo hoo!'.

"Maybe my gold coin is in that pool!" said Zuma. "Let's go and look, before those boys find it."

She was about to dart into the water when Tom saw something that made him grab

Zuma's shirt and pull her back.

From the opposite bank, two men with red handkerchiefs tied over their faces came bounding out of the woods. Before Tom could shout a warning, the men took the boys by surprise. With a sharp blow, they knocked them over and snatched up their entire haul of gold!

CHAPTER 3
ALL THAT GLITTERS

"That wasn't very nice!" cried Zuma. "We have to stop them before they get away!"

Tom glanced at the boys, who were struggling to climb out of the creek in their wet clothes. They'd never catch the robbers at that rate.

"C'mon!" Tom said. "Let's catch them!"

Zuma started running towards the men. Now Tom understood how she'd been able to escape from being sacrificed – this girl was fast! In seconds, she'd blocked the robbers' way. The men skidded to a stop, clearly surprised to see a young girl out in the middle of the wilderness.

Tom grabbed one of the boys' shovels from the bank of the creek, and ran to join Zuma. She was still blocking the robbers, who had now removed their handkerchiefs.

"Don't tell me you puny little runts are trying to stop us!" snorted the tall, skinny one. He had the biggest nose Tom had ever seen and long, greasy strands of hair inching over his forehead like earthworms. His face had a scar snaking all the way from his left ear to the middle of his upper lip.

"Out of the way, kids!" laughed his stout partner. This outlaw had blubbery cheeks and four chins. His beady eyes were so close together they almost looked crossed.

Big Nose took a step forward, but Zuma
stopped him by jumping on to his back and
tugging hard on his greasy hair. He was so
surprised by her attack that he staggered
and tripped, landing on a prickly cactus.
Tom swung his shovel into the back of the
other robber's knees, causing them to buckle
beneath him.

"Ouch!" the man croaked as he landed on his belly. "You'll regret that, boy!" He reached out and grabbed for Tom's ankle, but Chilli growled and nipped the man's thumb. He howled in pain.

By now, the two young prospectors had reached them. The older boy helped Zuma pin Big Nose to the ground. "That'll teach you to steal from honest, hardworking folk," he said.

"Get out of here," said the younger boy. "And don't let us see you sneaking round our claim again, do you hear?"

Zuma got off her captive and he hopped to his feet. But instead of leaving, the two outlaws pulled out guns and pointed them at the boys.

"Hand over your gold, or else!" ordered Big Nose.

The chubby outlaw snatched the boys' pans, then sneered at the contents. "Just a few measly flakes of gold," he spat.

"We don't need to waste our time with this, do we, Bob?" said Big Nose.

"We sure don't, Snake!" said Bob, shaking his head. "This time tomorrow we'll have us a whole coachload of gold!"

With that, the outlaws threw down the pans and hurried off into the woods.

"Thanks for that," said the taller boy, tipping his hat to Zuma and giving Tom a grin. "You kids sure are brave."

"My name's Joe Smith," said the younger boy. "And this here's my big brother, Fred."

Zuma smiled. "No problem. I'm Zuma, and this is Tom."

"What brings you to Deadwood?" asked Fred.

"We're searching for gold," said Zuma.

"So's everybody here in the Dakota Territory," Fred chuckled. "That's why they call it the Gold Rush. But you two are the youngest prospectors I've seen yet."

"Um, well, I guess you could say we're very mature for our age," Tom lied. "Besides, you're not much older than us. How did you come to be prospectors?"

A sad look flickered across both boys' faces.

"Our ma and pa passed away last spring," Joe explained with a catch in his voice. "So we came out here to find our fortune. We staked our claim legally, but claims are so scarce now, people are trying to take what isn't theirs. Fights are breaking out in Deadwood almost every night."

"Our claim is all we've got, and we're the only ones who should be panning here," added Fred. "So we're mighty thankful you two stepped in when you did," said Fred. "Where's your claim?"

"We don't have one," Tom said with a shrug.

"Well, then, you can share ours today," offered Joe. "It's the least we can do."

Zuma didn't need to be told twice. She was eager to find the first coin. She jumped in the water and began splashing around. Chilli followed right behind her. He paddled to the centre of the pool, yapping with excitement.

"Here, let me show you how to do it," Fred said with a chuckle.

For the next few hours, Fred and Joe taught Tom and Zuma how to dip their pans into the water and sift through the sand for golden flakes or nuggets. The sun had just reached its peak in the sky when Tom saw something glittering in his pan.

"Yes!" he cried out. "I've found gold!"

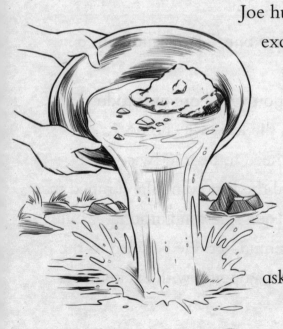

Joe hurried over and examined the gold flake in Tom's pan. "You sure did!" he confirmed. "It's real."

"Is it the coin?" Zuma asked hopefully.

Tom shook his head. "But we've only just started looking," he said.

A few minutes later, Zuma shrieked and held up a little gold lump. "I found some too!"

"Hey, that's a whole nugget," said Fred, impressed. "That'll be worth a few dollars for sure!"

Tom was glad Zuma had found gold. But big as the nugget was, they both knew it wouldn't get her any closer to freedom. And as the day wore on, though Tom and Zuma found a few more flakes of gold, there was no sign of the sun coin.

"You two did mighty fine for beginners," said Fred. "But we need to head back to town before the bank closes. And we don't want to be out on the streets after dark."

Tom and Zuma helped the boys pack up

their pickaxes, shovels and pans. They also offered the brothers the gold they'd found, since it wasn't much use to them. At first the boys refused, but Zuma insisted and finally Fred and Joe accepted with heartfelt thanks.

As they headed out of the woods, something occurred to Tom. "Why do we need to get to town before dark?" he asked.

"Because," said Fred in a serious voice, "we're going to Deadwood… the wildest town in the whole Wild West!"

CHAPTER 4

DEADWOOD

After a long, dusty walk, finally they reached Deadwood. Tom felt like he was on the set of an old cowboy film. The long main street was bustling with prospectors in dirty blue jeans and cowboys wearing chaps and spurs. The brightly painted buildings that lined the wooden sidewalk looked as if they'd been built in a hurry. The whole town was noisy with men shouting, carts rumbling and horses clip-clopping.

Zuma suddenly froze in her tracks. "What are those creatures with the swishy tails?" she gasped.

"They're called horses," Tom explained. "Haven't you seen one before?"

Zuma shook her head and jumped in fear as a passing horse let out a loud whinny.

"They're nothing to be afraid of," Tom said.

"Are you sure they won't eat me?" Zuma asked.

"Not unless you're a carrot or a sugar lump," Tom promised.

As the Smith brothers led them towards the bank, they passed a pretty young lady dressed in a hoop skirt.

"Why is her skirt so big?" Zuma asked. "Is

she hiding something?"

Tom laughed. "I don't think so. Even though you could almost park a truck underneath it. She's just trying to look trendy."

Zuma snorted. "How silly. You couldn't run very fast in a skirt like that."

The bank was at the end of the main street. Dirt-covered prospectors wandered in and out, carrying bags bulging with gold.

"Quick question," said Zuma, turning to face Tom. "How are we supposed to find one little gold coin in a place that's practically dripping with the stuff?"

Tom had been wondering the same thing himself.

Inside the bank, Fred gave his sack of gold to a teller, who weighed it then made some calculations. Moments later, Fred was holding a handful of paper money.

"Grub's on us, kids," he said.

They headed for the saloon, which was also the stagecoach station.

"The stagecoach goes all the way to Cheyenne," Joe explained, pointing at a fancy wagon parked outside. "Brings people who are hoping to get rich to Deadwood, and carries all the gold they find to the banks back East."

Zuma tucked Chilli under her arm and they entered the saloon through the swinging doors.

Inside, a jaunty tune tinkled from a piano. While Joe, Tom and Zuma found a table, Fred went up to the bar. Tom couldn't believe he was dining in a real Western saloon! His eyes scanned the room. There were a few ladies in hoop skirts, but most of

the people there were men – rough sorts who shouted jokes and insults at one another.

In the corner by a large window, four men were playing cards. The table was littered with empty bottles and stubbed-out cigars. A hefty pile of money sat in the middle. One of the card players wore a big white hat over his long red hair. He had a moustache that twirled up at the ends. Sitting next to him was a younger man with sharp blue eyes. The other two players looked to be farmers, one with a bushy beard, the other wearing dirty dungarees.

Moments later, Fred returned carrying four mugs.

"What's this?" Tom asked, looking at the dark liquid in his mug.

"It's sarsaparilla," Fred said. "Me and Joe love it."

Tom took a sip. It was sweet, and spicy too. The flavour was a bit like ginger beer, but lighter.

"I ordered us the daily special," said Fred. "Thanks to that big old nugget Zuma found, we can afford a feast!"

"I wish I'd found a big old Aztec coin instead," Zuma grumbled.

But Tom barely heard her. He'd just spotted a poster tacked up behind the bar that made his blood run cold. He was looking at a drawing of two outlaws. One had a giant nose and the other a jowly face. "Look!" he said. "It's the men who tried to rob you this morning!"

Joe scowled at the poster. "I ain't had much book learning, but I can read what it says: WANTED – DEAD OR ALIVE."

"Rattlesnake Ron and Blackheart Bob," Tom read aloud. "They robbed the St Louis stagecoach."

"What else does it say?" Joe prompted.

"It says they're armed…" Tom gulped "… and dangerous."

The barman appeared and plunked down

four steaming bowls. "Rabbit stew," he barked, then scratched his chin. "Least, I *think* it's rabbit. Sometimes it's hard to tell. Hope you kids like prairie dog!"

Chilli let out a whimper and hid under the table.

"Don't worry," said Zuma, patting Chilli's head. "I won't let anyone eat *you*."

"Remember how those outlaws boasted about having a coach filled with gold?" said Tom.

Zuma nodded.

"Well, I think they're planning to raid the Deadwood stagecoach tomorrow, just like they did in St Louis!"

"Are you sure?" Zuma asked.

"Almost," said Tom. He turned to Fred. "Does the stagecoach go straight through to Cheyenne?"

"No," said Fred. "It makes lots of stops. First one's Spring Creek."

Tom turned back to Zuma. "*Now* I'm sure! The riddle mentioned a Spring Creek. I bet your gold coin is going to be on that coach!"

"Where can I find the police department?" Tom asked the barman. "Or the sheriff's office?"

"We ain't got either of those things, son," the barman said. "But we *do* got us one of the greatest marshals ever to wear a badge."

"Then where can I find *him*?"

Before the barman could reply, there was a loud crash from the corner where the men were playing poker. The saloon's front window was completely shattered! The man with the moustache and white hat had just thrown the farmer with the beard right through it. The younger card player carried on rearranging his hand of cards, but the other farmer looked furious.

Oh boy, thought Tom. *This can't be good.* "Maybe we should fetch the marshal," he suggested.

The barman laughed. "That's what I was just about to tell you, son." He pointed to the card game. "That *is* the marshal!"

"What?!" Tom spun round and stared at the card players.

"That fella with blue eyes is the marshal, Wyatt Earp," the barman said. "The one with red hair swigging whisky is the famous lawman, Wild Bill Hickok."

Wild Bill was standing by the broken window, brushing off his hands. "I don't take kindly to men who cheat at cards," he said.

The farmer in the dirty dungarees seethed.

"You calling my friend a cheater, Hickok?" he snarled, spitting a squirt of tobacco juice on the floor.

"Darn right I am!"

"Those are fighting words!" hollered Dungarees.

Wyatt Earp just sat calmly, studying his cards.

The next moment, the farmer lunged at Wild Bill. Bill caught him by the front of his dungarees and flung him across the room, where he landed in a cowboy's stew. The cowboy hit him over the head with a bottle. A man at the next table picked up a wooden stool and tossed it at the cowboy.

"Quick," said Fred, "you kids, get under the table!"

They ducked just in time to miss the stool that came flying past. A brawl was now in full swing. Punches were thrown, furniture was smashed. Plates and glasses crashed to the floor. The piano player jumped up from his bench and ran for his life! Then…

Bang!

Bang!

Bang!

Three shots rang out, hitting a stuffed moose head mounted on the wall right between the eyes. The room came to a standstill as all eyes turned to Marshal Wyatt Earp. He remained calmly seated in his chair, holding his cards. But now he was holding a smoking pistol.

"I guess that's one way to stop a fight," Zuma observed.

A slow grin was spreading across Marshal Earp's face. "Four aces," he said, laying the cards on the table. "Beat you again, Hickok."

Wild Bill sighed. "I'll be more than happy

to settle up, Earp, but first you're gonna have to help me see this gentleman out."

The saloon was silent as the marshal stood. He put his gun in its holster, then sauntered to the opposite side of the table, where Bill was clutching the farmer in a headlock. Together, the lawmen tossed him out of the broken window, where he joined his bearded friend. Then Earp and Hickok shook hands and the crowd erupted into cheers.

Tom smiled. If anyone could catch Rattlesnake Ron and Blackheart Bob, it was these two! He removed his hat and nervously walked over. "Excuse me, Marshal Earp, Mr Wild Bill."

"Howdy, little fella," said Hickok, ruffling Tom's hair. "You must be new here in Deadwood."

"Just passing through," Tom told him.

"What can we do for you?" asked
Marshal Earp.

"You can help me stop a crime!"

Hickok was instantly on alert. Earp's hand
went to his holster.

"It's not going to happen until tomorrow,"
Tom continued. "Rattlesnake Ron and
Blackheart Bob are going to rob the

Deadwood stagecoach when it gets to Spring Creek!"

The lawmen exchanged an amused look and relaxed again. Tom felt his cheeks flush.

The next thing he knew, Zuma was standing beside him. "It's true!" she cried. "They said they were after a coachload of gold."

"Why, that just ain't possible, little lady," said Earp, nodding at the wagon outside. "That stagecoach is as safe as it can be. I hired the armed guards myself and Hickok here made sure the coach was fitted with every modern safety feature."

Tom guessed the marshal wasn't talking about an alarm system.

"The strongbox is impossible to break into," Wild Bill bragged.

"And it's fireproof," boasted Earp, puffing

out his chest. "There won't be any stage raids in these parts while *I'm* Deadwood's marshal." With that, the two lawmen ordered another round of drinks and started a new card game.

Tom and Zuma went back to their table and sat down, but neither felt like eating.

"We can't let those outlaws rob the stagecoach," said Zuma. "My freedom is at stake!"

"I know." Tom frowned and turned to the elder of the Smith brothers. "Fred, you said the first stop is Spring Creek, right?"

Fred nodded.

"What time does it leave Deadwood tomorrow?"

"Just before sunrise," Fred explained. "The driver needs a good night's sleep. In the morning, they'll hitch up six fresh horses and be on their way."

"That gives us plenty of time to get there," said Tom.

"What do you mean?" asked Joe, helping himself to Zuma's stew.

"I mean," said Tom, "if the stage is leaving for Spring Creek tomorrow, then Zuma and I are going today! If Wyatt Earp won't listen to me, maybe the marshal in the next town *will*!"

CHAPTER 5

YEE-HA!

"You want me to climb up on *that*?" Zuma's eyes were wide with terror as she stared up at the white horse. "You're joking!"

They were in the barn where the Smith brothers stabled their horses.

"How else are you going to ride it?" asked Tom.

"*Ride* it? You're out of your mind!"

"It's easy," said Joe, patting the white horse's side. "Lolly's a very gentle horse. Just don't say 'giddyup'. She knows I only say that when I want her to bolt."

"Hurry up, Zuma. Get on the horse!" said Tom impatiently.

Zuma narrowed her eyes. "I'm not a slave any more. Nobody tells me what to do!"

Tom sighed. "The only way we can get to Spring Creek in time to stop the robbery is if we ride horses. Fred and Joe have been kind enough to lend us theirs. So would you *please* get on the saddle so we can go!"

Fred lifted Zuma up. She swung one leg over Lolly's back and missed the saddle entirely, sliding down the other side of the horse and landing in the dirt.

Joe hurried to help her, but Zuma swatted him away. Brushing herself off, she put one foot in the stirrup and swung herself on to the saddle. This time she managed to stay on.

Joe showed Zuma how to squeeze her ankles gently into the horse's sides to make her walk on. Then he showed her how to use the reins to tell Lolly whether to go fast or slow, or which way to turn.

Tom mounted Fred's big chestnut horse, Cannonball. He'd ridden horses during his previous time-travel adventures, but he knew that every horse was different. "Why's he called Cannonball?" he asked Fred nervously.

"Because he moves as fast as one," laughed Fred. "But he sure doesn't like the sound of one," he continued. "Loud noises make him buck."

Tom held the reins tightly.

While Fred gave Tom directions to Spring Creek, Joe tied two bedrolls behind the saddle. Then he filled Cannonball's saddlebags with supplies – a canteen of water, beef jerky, bacon and some biscuits. The only thing in Lolly's saddlebag was Chilli.

"Good luck! Be careful!" called Fred and Joe, waving.

Tom made a clicking sound with his tongue to get Cannonball moving. Zuma copied the noise, and Lolly followed at a slow walk.

"Just hold on to those reins," Tom reminded her, as they left Deadwood behind. "And whatever you do, don't say you-know-what."

Zuma rolled her eyes. "I'm not a complete idiot. I know I'm not supposed to say 'Giddyup'."

Lolly took off like lightning, her hooves kicking up clouds of dust.

"Oh no!" Tom pressed his horse into a

gallop and raced after them.

Up ahead, Zuma had lost her stirrups
and was clinging on to Lolly's neck. Luckily,
Cannonball was speedy and quickly caught
them up.

"Pull back on the reins," Tom shouted to Zuma. "Yell, 'Whoa'!"

"Whoa, Lolly!" Zuma screamed. "Whhhhoooaaa!"

Lolly obeyed immediately, slowing to a stop. Tom rode up to Zuma, expecting her to be upset. But Zuma turned to him with a big grin on her face.

"That was fun! Let's ride all the way to Spring Creek like that."

"I don't think the horses could handle it," laughed Tom.

They rode across the open prairie until the sun began to set.

"Let's break and make camp," Tom suggested, tying the horses to a tree. "I wish we could start a fire but I don't think Joe gave us any matches."

Zuma smiled. "You just unroll those

sleepy-baggy-thingies and leave the fire to me."

As Tom smoothed out the bedrolls, Zuma collected sticks and twigs. She made a circle of stones in the dirt and arranged the sticks like a tiny teepee. Then she began rubbing two twigs together very quickly. There was a wisp of smoke, followed by a spark and, finally, a flame.

"Brilliant!" said Tom.

They shared a meal of bacon and biscuits, and watched the stars appear in the sky.

"It's funny," said Zuma, smiling up at the velvety black canopy. "So many things have changed since my time, but the stars still look the same."

"That's kind of cool," said Tom.

"For us Aztecs," Zuma continued, "the night sky is ruled by the most important god of all—Tezcatlipoca."

Tom crawled into his sleeping bag and looked over at Zuma. She looked snug and cosy in her bag, with Chilli lying across her feet, resting his little face on his paws.

Tom was just drifting off to sleep when a chorus of bloodcurdling howls ripped through the night. He sat up, heart pounding. Zuma, however, was perfectly calm.

"It's just coyotes howling at the moon," she said. "Don't worry. The fire will keep them away." Chilli let out an indignant bark and Zuma giggled. "Chilli will protect us from them too, won't you, little pup?"

Tom had his doubts about Chilli protecting them from anything bigger than a rabbit but he didn't say so. Tom felt wide awake again. "Tell me about your life in Mexico," he said to Zuma.

"I was a kitchen slave to a nobleman," Zuma told him. "I worked hard every day. My job was cooking. That's why I know how to start a fire. Then one day my master offered me up as a sacrifice to please the gods."

"Wow. You must have been a really rubbish cook."

Zuma laughed. "That wasn't the reason. It was because I was always trying to run away. All I ever wanted was to know the feeling of freedom."

Freedom was something Tom never thought much about, simply because he'd always had it. He couldn't imagine belonging to someone, especially someone who could sentence him to death. It just wasn't right. "We're going to find those coins, Zuma," he promised. "All six of them. Then you'll be able to go home and be free."

"Thank you," Zuma whispered.

The coyotes howled again, but this time Tom wasn't afraid. Moments later, they were both fast asleep.

They rose at sunrise and set off for Spring Creek. Tom was amazed by the size of the Black Hills rolling away beyond the grasslands.

"Um… what's *that*?" asked Zuma, pointing to a cloud billowing across the plain. They were riding along a path at the edge of a deep ravine.

Tom squinted, fearing it was Tlaloc's magic mist coming to take them away before they'd found the coin. But then he realised the cloud was dust being kicked up by a herd of huge cows with long, pointy horns.

"It's a cattle drive!" he said, eyes lighting up. "Cool!"

As they drew closer, Tom and Zuma could see the cowboys on horseback. One man was spinning a rope lasso above his head. Tom watched in awe as the cowboy flicked his wrist to land the hoop round the head of a runaway bull. The cowboy tightened the circle round the animal's neck and led the bull back to the herd.

"What's this all about?" asked Zuma. "Are they taking their pet cows for a walk?"

Tom laughed. "Sort of. They're taking them to a different place to graze. They go for miles at a time. It can be really danger—"

He was interrupted by a loud clap of thunder. The cowboys looked up at the clear blue sky, confused. The cattle also noticed this sudden change in the weather. A few snorted and stamped their hooves.

"Uh-oh," said Zuma.

"This is NOT supposed to be fun!" came Tlaloc's voice from the sky. The thunder startled Cannonball, who reared up, but Tom managed to stay in the saddle. Inside Lolly's saddlebag, Chilli quivered with fear and covered his ears with his paws.

"You have not been sent through time to enjoy the scenery," Tlaloc scolded from the clouds. "I clearly need to make your challenge harder."

And with that there was another, louder roll of thunder over the plain, and this time the cattle were spooked. The ground trembled as the frightened animals began to run. Suddenly, the entire herd were heading straight towards Tom and Zuma.

"Stampede!" shouted Tom.

"What do we do?" cried Zuma.

They were trapped – the cattle coming at them from one direction, the deep ravine on the other. There was no chance they could ride their horses safely down such a steep drop. Their only hope was to get the herd to change direction. But how? Tom thought back to every nature programme he'd ever seen and every cowboy story he'd ever read, but none of them had prepared him for this.

Then it hit him – if the sound of thunder had frightened the cattle into running *this* way, maybe another loud noise could scare them into running in the *opposite* direction.

"Make some noise!" he shouted to Zuma. "Be as loud as you can!"

Instantly she let out an ear-piercing scream, then another and another. Tom began to clap his hands and sing at the top

of his lungs. 'Old MacDonald' was the only
song he could think of under such pressure.
Even Chilli pitched in by barking as loudly as
he could.

It wasn't working. The cattle were getting
closer. Tom could see the pointy tips of their
horns aiming right at them. Suddenly, a shrill
noise pierced the air. Zuma had two fingers

in her mouth and was blowing. Her whistle
was so loud that Tom had to cover his ears.

In a massive blur of hide and horn, the
herd swung itself round and ran the other
way. The cowboys chased them at top speed,
twirling their lassos and shouting, "Hyah!
Hyah!"

It worked! Tom let out a long, relieved

breath and uncovered his ears.

One of the cowboys galloped over to tip his hat in appreciation. "Thank you kindly, pardners," he said. "You saved the herd. They'd have died if they'd gone over the ravine."

"Us too," Tom added. "But you're welcome."

The cowboy spurred his horse and rode off in a cloud of dust.

Tom and Zuma waited until the herd was well out of sight before moving on, just in case Tlaloc had any ideas about spooking them again. Tom realised that the rain god was not going to make Zuma's quest easy. They would have to be careful and stay alert!

"We'd better get going," he said, when the dusty cloud of the cattle drive had disappeared over the horizon. "We've lost a

lot of time. The stagecoach will be getting
close to Spring Creek." He grinned at Zuma.
"Think you can handle riding at a faster
pace?"

Zuma winked. "I've got one word for
you," she said, gathering up her reins.
"*Giddyup!*"

CHAPTER 6
STAGECOACH STICK-UP

They rode hard and fast across the prairie.

Unfortunately, not fast enough.

Tom heard a faint rattling behind him. As the sound grew closer, he looked over his shoulder and saw the Deadwood stagecoach rushing along, unaware of the trouble it was heading towards.

"Hey!" Tom shouted to the driver. "Hey, slow down! Wait! You can't go to Spring Creek! You're in danger!"

But his voice was drowned out by the clatter of wheels and the horse's hooves. Even as Tom screamed, the driver waved and smiled, thinking Tom was just being friendly. Tom was shocked to see that the two armed guards sitting beside the driver were both fast asleep.

"Stop!" shouted Zuma. "There are robbers ahead!"

But the coach, with its team of six powerful horses, easily overtook them. It flew past without a second glance, hurtling towards Spring Creek.

As the coach approached a rocky outcrop, two men with big hats and red handkerchiefs tied round their faces jumped out from behind a big boulder, waving their pistols. One was tall and thin, the other was short and plump. Even from this distance, Tom was pretty sure he knew who they were.

The stagecoach came to such an abrupt stop that both guards were thrown from the driver's box. Loud bangs rang out, as the criminals fired off warning shots and shouted orders. Tom could just make out the driver raising his hands in the air as the passengers stepped out of the coach, holding their hands up too.

"We've got to help them!" cried Zuma.

"Those outlaws have guns," Tom pointed out. "They'll see us coming and shoot."

"But—"

"Putting ourselves in danger isn't going to help those stagecoach passengers," said Tom firmly.

Feeling helpless, they watched from a distance as Ron and Bob tied up the passengers, the driver and the guards and climbed into the driver's box, firing a few more bullets into the sky. Then the stagecoach took off again.

"Now what?" asked Zuma.

In response, Tom cried, "Giddyup!" and flicked his horse's reins. Zuma did the same.

They rode up to the bound and gagged passengers, and quickly untied the stagecoach driver.

"Release the others," Tom told him. "Then head on to Spring Creek. We'll get help!"

Then they rode off at full speed, following the dusty road. Before long, Tom caught sight of the stagecoach in the distance. Urging their horses on, Tom and Zuma rode up right behind it.

Gesturing wildly with one hand, Tom signalled to Zuma to stay hidden behind the stagecoach. For a moment he wondered whether they could somehow jump on, but he knew it was far too risky – get it wrong and they'd break their necks.

Over the noise of the galloping horses and the stagecoach's rattling wheels, Tom could only hear bits of the outlaws' conversation.

"Why do you always get to be the driver?" Rattlesnake complained. "I never get to drive!"

"That's because you drive like my great-granny!" Blackheart snapped.

The stagecoach rocketed on, bumping over large rocks and racing through deep gulleys. Bob was so reckless, there were moments when Tom thought the whole wagon might tip over. His arms ached from holding on to the reins, and his legs were sore from bouncing up and down in the saddle. He could feel blisters beginning to form on his hands. He hoped the stagecoach would come to a stop soon.

After a few miles the road suddenly veered sharply to the left. The turn was so tight that the coach tipped up on to two wheels. It rolled on, then slammed back down with a loud bang.

The noise startled Cannonball. The big horse reared, waving his front legs in the

air. Tom clung to the reins, but his terrified
mount bucked in fright.

"Aaarrgh!" screamed Tom as he flew
through the air.

He squeezed his eyes shut and braced
himself to hit the hard, rocky ground.

CHAPTER 7

A SHOT IN THE DARK

Instead of landing with a crash, Tom hit the ground with a *SPLASH*! By a stroke of luck, he had landed in a soft, muddy ditch.

Tom scrambled to his feet and wiped the mud out of his eyes.

Zuma laughed. "You're so muddy you look like you've been dipped in chocolate," she said.

"Says the girl who's normally painted blue," Tom replied with a grin. He walked carefully over to Cannonball, who was now calmly drinking water from a puddle. "We'd better get going again," he said.

"Maybe we should walk," said Zuma. She pointed up ahead, to where the stagecoach had turned off the road and was heading into the woods. She swung one leg over her saddle and jumped down to the ground.

After tying their exhausted horses to a tree, Tom and Zuma set off on foot. They had no trouble keeping up with the stagecoach as it struggled slowly through the low-hanging branches and thick undergrowth. When the coach came to a halt in a clearing, Tom and Zuma hid behind a tall pine tree and peeked round the trunk. Rattlesnake Ron had flung open the stagecoach door and was searching inside, cackling over the purses and wallets the passengers had left behind.

But Blackheart Bob was only interested in one thing. He pulled out a large metal box with a heavy padlock from a shelf beneath the driver's box and threw it to the ground. He found a thick tree branch and swung it at the lock. Four heavy blows was all it took to break the lock in two.

Tom shook his head, thinking that Wyatt Earp had seriously overestimated the coach's 'safety features'. Then Blackheart opened the box and Tom saw a flash of gold!

There were piles and piles of big gold bars. Tom couldn't imagine what it must be worth. There were also a few large golden nuggets.

"Yee-ha!" cawed Blackheart Bob, pulling out a handful of gold bars. "We're rich, Snake! Let's have ourselves a drink to celebrate."

Rattlesnake opened a bottle of whisky. "I get the first swig!"

"No, *I* get the first swig!"

"That ain't fair. You got to drive!"

"I know how we'll decide," said Blackheart. He reached back into the metal box and pulled out a piece of gold that gleamed more brightly than all the other bars and nuggets combined. "Let's flip a *coin*!"

Tom and Zuma looked at each other, eyes wide. Tom held his breath as Bob flipped the coin. As it spun in the air, it caught a ray of sunshine, lighting up the Aztec sun on its face. Zuma was about to squeal with delight but Tom clapped his hand over her mouth just in time.

"We have to get that coin," she hissed.

"Let's wait until it's safe," Tom whispered back.

While Blackheart and Rattlesnake guzzled a bottle of whisky, Tom and Zuma hid behind the tree. They took turns holding Chilli and scratching him behind his ears. Before long, the outlaws' voices began to sound tired.

"That Wyatt Earp's no match for us," boasted Rattlesnake, yawning. "I bet that pretty dancing girl, Clementine, will marry me now that I'm rich!"

"That pretty dancing girl can't stand the sight of you," Blackheart laughed. Then he belched. "Forget her, Snake, and buy yourself a ranch instead."

Rattlesnake's answer was a loud snore.

Bob sighed and then also closed his eyes.

Soon after, he also began to snore.

"Perfect," whispered Tom. "They're sound asleep. Now all we have to do is grab the coin and make a run for it." Tom and Zuma stepped out from behind the tree and tiptoed towards the sleeping outlaws. Slowly, silently they moved forward until …

CRACK!

Tom froze. He'd stepped on a twig. Next to him, Zuma gasped in fear. They both dropped to the ground, hoping their muddy clothes would help them blend into the undergrowth.

Blackheart sputtered awake. "Wha-waz-that?" he slurred, fumbling for his holster. He wobbled to his feet. "Wake up, Snake! Somebody's shooting at us!"

Rattlesnake Ron made a grunting noise.

Without checking whether his partner was

injured, Blackheart Bob gathered up as much gold as he could carry before unhitching one of the horses. Seconds later, Tom and Zuma heard the clatter of hooves galloping out of the woods.

When Rattlesnake Ron let out a loud snore, Tom let out the breath he hadn't even realised he was holding.

He and Zuma stood up slowly and tiptoed towards the box full of gold. Tom lifted the lid and it creaked loudly.

Rattlesnake Ron stirred, rolled over and threw one long arm over the box. He snuggled up to it and grabbed Tom's hand, muttering, "Oh, Clementine!"

"Oh no," Tom moaned softly. "I can't open the box now!"

"I have an idea," Zuma whispered. "Don't move!"

"I *can't* move," Tom whispered back.

Rattlesnake Ron squeezed Tom's hand tightly. "Oh, you have such a dainty hand, my darling Clementine," he muttered sleepily.

Tom watched nervously as Zuma tiptoed back towards the tree they had hidden behind. She picked up a fallen branch from the ground. Creeping back to Rattlesnake Ron, she used it to tickle the bandit's chin. Tom could only stare. What was she doing?

After a few seconds, Ron let out a sleepy giggle and gently swatted at the branch.

Zuma continued to brush it against Rattlesnake's cheek.

"Aww, come on, Clementine," Rattlesnake mumbled. "That tickles." He dropped Tom's hand and, chuckling in his sleep, turned over.

"Now," hissed Zuma. "Hurry!"

Tom quickly looked in the box. There were still piles of gold bars, but the sun coin was gone. He turned to Zuma and shook his head. "It's not there, and Blackheart Bob could have gone anywhere!" He kicked the dirt in frustration.

But Zuma grabbed Tom's arm and pointed. A rolled-up piece of parchment was sticking out of Rattlesnake's pocket. Slowly and carefully she slid it out. She unrolled the paper and revealed a map.

Zuma held the map up to the moonlight, and Tom saw that it showed a prairie south of Deadwood. A big red X was marked at the entrance to a place called Wind Cave.

"That must be where he's gone," said Zuma. "Let's follow him!"

Tom shook his head. "No. It's too risky. He might still have his gun. Let's go back to Deadwood and get Wyatt Earp and Wild Bill to help us. It's their job, after all."

"But that will take ages. I think we can handle him ourselves," Zuma protested. "There're two of us. You can distract him and I can snatch the coin."

"That coin won't do you any good if you get shot," said Tom.

"OK," huffed Zuma. "But let's hurry!"

Zuma gathered what remained of the

gold as proof, while Tom quickly tied up
Rattlesnake Ron with rope.

"What are you doing, Clementine?"
muttered Ron, as Tom tightened the rope
round his feet. "Hey!" Ron suddenly
woke up. "You're not Clementine!" Then,

struggling to get free, he shouted, "You'll pay for this! Nobody messes with Rattlesnake Ron and lives to tell the tale!"

Pushing aside branches and fighting their way through the undergrowth, Tom and Zuma made it back to Lolly and Cannonball.

Zuma put Chilli in her saddlebag, then they mounted the horses and galloped back to Deadwood, with Rattlesnake Ron's threats ringing out in the night.

CHAPTER 8
ROUND UP A POSSE

Tom and Zuma rode hard and reached
Deadwood at dawn. They found Wyatt Earp
on the outskirts of town, cracking his whip at a
line of empty bottles balanced on a fence. Each
time he snapped the whip, the top of a bottle
would shatter clean off. He never missed.

"That's amazing," said Tom, jumping
down from his horse.

"Thanks, son. I reckon I could whip a
bumblebee right out of the sky if I had to,"

Marshal Earp chuckled. "Not that I'd ever
have to."

"Marshal Earp, please…" panted Zuma
as she dismounted "… you have to help us."
In one long rush, she filled him in on all that

had happened in Spring Creek, and how Blackheart Bob had escaped with gold from the Deadwood stagecoach.

"They have something very valuable that belongs to my friend," Tom finished, handing over the recovered gold. "We have to get it back."

Wyatt coiled his bull whip and hung it on his belt. "What we need is a posse to search for Blackheart Bob. I'll round up some men and we'll be on our way. You can wait here in Deadwood—"

"But we want to be part of the posse," Zuma cried, looking panic-stricken. "We have to be!"

"She's right," said Tom. "Please, sir. Let us come with you."

Wyatt Earp laughed. "You're just a couple of kids!"

"A couple of kids with a map," Tom corrected, holding up the parchment.

The next thing Tom and Zuma knew, they were heading back the way they had come. Only this time, Wyatt Earp, Wild Bill Hickok and Fred and Joe Smith were riding along with them.

"I still think these young 'uns should have stayed home," grumbled Wild Bill. "This is dangerous business."

"I told you, Hickok," snapped Earp, "we *had* to bring 'em! They wouldn't give me the darn map!"

Grinning, Tom led the way across the prairie to Wind Cave. The vast land was bathed in pale pink and yellow light. Wildflowers bobbed in the swaying grass, and furry little gophers peeked out of their holes to watch the riders hurry past.

When they reached the mouth of the cave, everyone secured their horses, and Hickok lit a lantern to light their way.

The Smith brothers hesitated. "I've heard about this cave," Fred whispered. "It goes

on for miles, like a big ol' labyrinth deep
beneath the prairie. Heard the Sioux people
think this is a sacred place." He shuddered.
"No wonder. Sure seems like a good place to
bury the dead."

"I've heard it said these caves are filled with angry ghosts and spirits," Joe added, nodding.

"Afraid of some silly little bedtime stories?" laughed Wild Bill. "Come on!" He ducked inside the cave, and the others followed.

Tom, Zuma and Chilli crept through the darkness, following the flickering shadows cast by the lantern. When Tom ran his fingers along the cave's walls, he was surprised to find that it had lots of small holes in it. It felt a bit like a rocky sponge. A rush of air and a loud flapping sound caused them all to jump... even Hickok! Tom looked up to see a whole colony of bats sweeping out of the darkness. Wild Bill covered his head with his hands and screamed.

It was Joe's turn to laugh. "Afraid of some silly little bats, Wild Bill?"

Bill snorted and the posse continued on. The walls of the cave narrowed and twisted as they went further and further inside.

Suddenly, the whole cave began to echo with a ghoulish moaning sound.

"What in heaven is that?" gasped Earp.

"Ghosts!" cried Joe and Fred together.

Wild Bill was trembling too hard to say anything.

The howling came again, sounding even scarier. Wyatt dropped the lantern and the two lawmen and the Smith brothers turned and ran for the cave's exit.

"Let's get out of here!" cried Zuma.

"No!" said Tom. "It's not spirits. It's just the wind. The way it travels through the cave makes it sound like groaning ghosts."

"I guess that's why they call it Wind Cave," reasoned Zuma.

"I think we're close." Tom picked up the lantern to shine it on the map. "A few more metres, then a left turn. I'm pretty sure that's where the hideout is."

"Your shadow looks like a monster," Zuma giggled, pointing to the huge, scary-looking shadow that the lantern cast on the cave's wall.

"Grrrr!" growled Tom, raising his arms above his head and curling his hands so they looked like claws.

He led the way deeper into the tunnel. Just as they turned into the next passageway, they heard a strange sound. They followed the noise to the end of the passage, which opened up into a wider space – the outlaws' hideout.

Peering into the gloom, Tom could just make out Blackheart Bob. He was curled up on the ground and looked scared. Beside him was his sack of gold.

"Oh, I been real bad," Bob babbled, stroking the sack of gold. "I been greedy, and now all them bad deeds are coming back to haunt me! The authorities shot Snake, and I just left him there. They're after me, I can feel it in my bones! If they catch me, I'll go to prison, but if I stay here, I'll rot without food and water." He let out a wail. "Why didn't I remember to take my gun!"

Zuma's eyes twinkled. "Let's see if we can make his fear work in our favour."

"How?" said Tom.

Zuma took the lantern and tiptoed round to Tom's other side. "Hold Chilli in front of the lantern." Chilli tugged on Tom's trousers with his teeth. Tom picked up the dog and held him in front of the light, casting an

enormous, dog-shaped shadow on the wall.
Tom grinned at Zuma. "Good plan!" he
whispered.

Chilli bared his teeth and growled. In
the cave, his normally yappy bark sounded
terrifying.

"A coyote!" gasped Blackheart Bob. The
outlaw jumped up, grabbed his bag of gold
and ran right past Tom and Zuma, who
ducked into a recess in the cave wall. They
gave chase, catching up with the outlaw just
as he reached the mouth of the cave... where
the posse waited with weapons drawn.

Wyatt Earp, Wild Bill Hickok and the
Smith brothers pointed their guns straight at
Blackheart Bob. But Blackheart wasn't ready
to surrender yet. He turned to run back into
the cave but, seeing Tom and Zuma behind
him, he reached out and grabbed them,

pulling them in front of him like a human
shield.

Tom gulped as he stared down the barrels
of four gleaming guns. And two of them were
in the hands of the sharpest shooters in the
Wild West!

CHAPTER 9

SHOWDOWN AT HIGH NOON

"Go ahead and shoot me!" Blackheart taunted, sneering at the lawmen. "But you'll have to go through these brats to do it." He ducked down behind Tom and Zuma and let out a wicked laugh. He pulled out a knife from his boot and held it to Tom's throat. "I ain't afraid of you, Mr Wyatt *Twerp*!"

Tom gulped as he felt the cold metal blade touching his throat. He froze, staring straight ahead in terror. His gaze fell on the bull whip, dangling from Wyatt's belt. Hadn't he boasted that his whip skills were so sharp he could whip a bee right out of the sky? Tom could only hope that Wyatt's aim was as good as he'd bragged it was!

"Hey, Marshal Earp," Tom called out. "Don't *bee* scared. Just tell this guy to *buzz* off."

The marshal looked at him as if he'd gone crazy. Tom tried again. If he came right out and said it, his plan wouldn't work.

"You might just have to *wing* it, sir. But please hurry. I'm so nervous, I'm about to break out in *hives*!"

Zuma caught on and joined in. "If you save us, it will be one *sweet* rescue," she said. "So whatever you do, don't *bumble* it up."

At last, realisation dawned. In a flash Earp's hand went to his belt and he snatched

the whip. The leather rope
whizzed through the air,
missing Tom's ear by a hair
and *thwacking* the knife right
out of Blackheart's hand.

Tom and Zuma broke out of the outlaw's grasp just as the posse rushed forward, surrounding Blackheart Bob and tying him up. Fred dragged the outlaw over to Wild Bill's horse and helped the lawman sling the thief belly-first across the horse's rump.

"Not the most comfortable way to travel," Fred observed, chuckling.

"Sure ain't," Bill agreed. "'Specially since I plan on making this a real *wild* ride!"

Wyatt Earp was examining Blackheart's bag of gold. "You know, there's a big old bounty on this bandit's head," he told Tom and Zuma. "And I think you two have earned it. When we get back to Deadwood, you kids will have a big reward coming to you."

"Thanks," said Zuma. "But we weren't planning to go back to Deadwood. And besides, all we really want is that." She pointed at the Aztec sun coin, glittering at the top of the bag.

Wyatt Earp tossed Zuma the coin, and she caught it, clutching it tightly in her fist.

"Can you give the rest of the reward to the Smith brothers?" asked Tom.

"Don't see why not," said Wyatt, turning to the boys. "I'll see to it you get the money as soon as we return to Deadwood. It's a hefty sum. More than you could ever make from your claim."

"Oh no!" protested Fred. "We can't take your money!"

"Don't worry," said Zuma. "We don't need it where we're going."

Fred smiled at Tom and Zuma. "That's mighty kind of you. Now I can set up a farm like I always wanted, and Joe can get on with his schooling."

"Schooling?" Joe gave his brother a sulky look. "I want to be a lawman."

"Tell you what, son," said Marshal Earp. "If you promise to go to school during the week, I'll make you my honorary deputy on the weekends. You're a brave boy, and the Wild West needs all the heroes it can get."

"How do we go back?" Zuma asked Tom, staring down at the coin.

"Same way we got here, I think," Tom replied, taking Zuma's hand. The sound of thunder ripped through the sky. A thick white cloud of mist swirled from the ground and wrapped itself around Zuma and Tom. Chilli ran to Zuma, who lifted him up and held him close.

"I know this is the Wild West," drawled Wyatt, "but doggone it, this is the wildest thing I've seen yet!"

Those were the last words Tom heard before the mysterious power swept in, pulling them back through time and space.

CHAPTER 10

JUST DESSERTS

Tom felt the smooth tile of the museum floor beneath his feet. He wriggled his toes inside his trainers, which had replaced his cowboy boots. Zuma, who had landed on her bottom in the treasure chest with her legs dangling over the side, was painted blue again. Her feathered headdress sat tilted on her head.

"*Oof!* Are the landings always this bumpy?" Zuma asked.

"'Fraid so," said Tom, helping her out of

the chest. They had to search a bit for Chilli,
who had landed in a clay urn. The little dog
seemed bewildered but unharmed.

Tom was just about to pick up Tlaloc's
drum when his dad returned from taking his

phone call. While Tom and Zuma had been having their Wild West adventure, time had stood still in the present day. Dad walked right past Zuma without seeing her, which made Tom chuckle. It was hard to believe that a blue girl covered in feathers could go unnoticed, but then again, this was magic.

"That drum belonged to the Aztec rain god, Tlaloc," Dad said.

"I think I might have heard of him," Tom said innocently.

Zuma giggled but Dad took no notice – he couldn't hear her, either.

"The Aztecs regularly sacrificed children to Tlaloc." Dad frowned at the drum. "It's horrible to us, of course, but the Aztecs saw it as a great honour to die on the altar in exchange for rainy weather."

"It was an honour this Aztec could do

without," said Zuma, crossing her arms over her chest.

Tom didn't blame her, but since his dad was there he couldn't say so.

As Dad crossed the room to unpack more of the exhibits, a thunderclap sounded and driving rain began to fall. Dad didn't seem to notice, and carried on with his work. Tlaloc's rain was obviously an illusion too.

Lightning flashed and suddenly the Aztec god was standing in the gallery. His eyes bulged and he looked even angrier than ever as he bared his sharp fangs at them.

"I have something for you," said Zuma. Smiling, she splashed through the puddles on the floor and presented the gold coin to Tlaloc.

"One down, five to go," said Tom.

"Yes," growled Tlaloc, accepting the coin

with a scowl. "You have surprised me…
this time. Perhaps I made your mission too
easy."

Zuma put her hands on her hips. "Or
maybe we're just really brave and clever."

"We'll see about that!" Tlaloc roared.
He opened his mouth to laugh, but the
sound that came out was another explosion
of thunder. He raised his hands and
immediately vanished in a shimmer of blue
water. The moment the god was gone, the
rain stopped falling. The puddles instantly
dried up and everything was back to
normal. Well, more or less. There was still
a blue, feathered Aztec girl in the museum.

"Let's head home," said Dad. "I'll
just gather my things and meet you
outside."

When Dad left, Tom turned to Zuma,

whose lip had begun to tremble.

She looked heartbroken. "You're leaving?"

"Yes," said Tom, nodding. "And so are you. There are five more sun coins out there and the only way to find them is if we work together."

Zuma grinned. "I like the sound of that."

Later that night, after Tom had tried explaining everything from cars to computers to what the toilet was used for, he left Zuma in his room and briefly disappeared. When he returned, he was carrying a tray with two steaming mugs of hot chocolate.

"I know the Aztecs drank this," he said. "I thought having some before bed might make you a little less homesick."

"Hate to break it to you," said Zuma, "but slaves rarely get homesick since 'home' is the place where people order us about."

Tom laughed and handed her a mug. "Well, maybe you'd like some anyway."

Zuma took a sip and her eyes widened in surprise. "This is delicious! Way better than Aztec hot chocolate!"

This surprised Tom. "Isn't the kind you drink at home delicious?"

"Not really. It's actually kind of watery and bitter. This is much nicer."

"Hmm. Well, I guess we *have* had five hundred years to improve it," Tom reasoned.

They laughed and clinked their mugs together in a toast.

"To time travel," said Tom. "I wonder where Tlaloc will send us next."

"Wherever it is," sighed Zuma, "I hope we don't run into anyone like Rattlesnake Ron and Blackheart Bob again."

Tom was almost certain that they would. He shivered, partly out of fear, but also from excitement. Time travel was dangerous but he was getting to see things that other kids could only dream about. He'd panned for gold, galloped across the prairie, and met real cowboys.

"We're definitely in for a rough ride," he said. "But I think we've proved that between the two of us we can think on our feet and get the job done."

Chilli barked and jumped up on the bed, wagging his tail. Zuma picked up the little dog and gave him a cuddle. "I think you

mean the *three* of us," she said, giggling, as
Chilli licked her face. "Together, we're an
unbeatable team."

Tom pretended to tip an imaginary
cowboy hat. "You said it, pardner."

TURN THE PAGE TO . . .

➤ Meet the REAL Cowboys!

➤ Find out fantastic FACTS!

➤ Battle with your GAMING CARDS!

➤ And MUCH MORE!

WHO WERE THE MIGHTIEST COWBOYS?

Wyatt Earp was a *real* lawman. Find out more about him and other famous Wild West lawmen and cowboys!

WYATT EARP was a marshal in several frontier towns. After a stagecoach robbery, Earp got into a famous feud with a local rancher who knew the robbers' identities. Their gunfight at the O.K. Corral lasted only 30 seconds but the shootout killed three cowboys and injured three more. Wyatt Earp was the only person who wasn't hurt! The outlaws took revenge, killing Earp's brothers, and Wyatt Earp hit back. Some saw him as a hero, some as a villain for taking the law into his own hands.

COWBOYS

WYATT EARP

Brain Power	300
Fear Factor	285
Bravery	320
Weapon: Bullwhip	330
TOTAL 1235	

WILD BILL HICKOK's real name was James Butler Hickok. He had many jobs before becoming a lawman, from driving a stagecoach to being a soldier during the American Civil War. He was involved in many famous shootouts. His legendary duels and rowdy attitude earned him the nickname 'Wild Bill'. He also showed off his shooting skills in Wild West shows with Buffalo Bill. In 1876, he was shot dead during a poker game. The cards he was holding when he died – a pair of black aces and a pair of black eights – are now called 'the dead man's hand'. Unlucky for some.

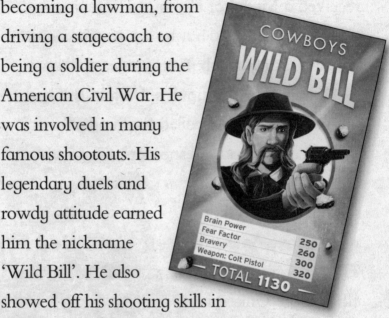

COWBOYS
WILD BILL

Brain Power	
Fear Factor	250
Bravery	260
Weapon: Colt Pistol	300
	320

TOTAL 1130

BUFFALO BILL worked as a scout for the US army when he was young, for which he received a Medal of Honour. His real name was William Cody, but he got his nickname while working as a buffalo hunter, killing 4,280 buffalo in 18 months. Buffalo Bill had his own circus show called Buffalo Bill's Wild West. It featured shooters, displays of horsemanship and re-enactments of battles with Native Americans. The show toured all over the United States and Europe, making Buffalo Bill a celebrity. Yee-ha!

COWBOYS
BUFFALO BILL

Brain Power	190
Fear Factor	220
Bravery	250
Weapon: Winchester Rifle	300

TOTAL 960

BILLY THE KID was born in New York City.
When he was 15 he
became an orphan and
joined a gang of outlaws
called The Regulators.
When The Regulators'
leader was killed, the
gang took revenge by
killing Sheriff Brady,
which led to a four-
day gunfight. Billy

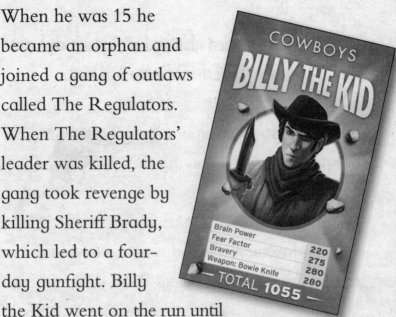

the Kid went on the run until
he was caught and sentenced to death. He
escaped from prison, but was tracked down
and killed by Sheriff Patrick Garrett, who
wrote a book called *The Authentic Life of Billy
the Kid*, turning the young outlaw into hero.
According to legend, Billy the Kid killed 21
men – one for each year of his life!

WEAPONS

Wyatt Earp was an expert whip-cracker! Find out what other weapons lawmen used in the Wild West.

Colt Pistol: a metallic handgun with a revolving cylinder containing multiple chambers. Commonly used by lawmen, cowboys and also soldiers during the American Civil War.

Winchester Rifle: an early 'repeating rifle', popular during the Wild West era and used by lawmen, cowboys and settlers – for hunting and as a weapon.

Bowie knife: a fixed-blade knife, originally designed to be a wearable, close-combat weapon – to replace longer swords. It was 8-12 inches in length and had a heavy blade.

Bullwhip: a single-tailed whip, usually made of braided leather. It was originally used to control large herds of livestock, such as cattle, when out in open country.

WILD WEST TIMELINE

In COWBOY SHOWDOWN Tom and Zuma go to the Wild West.
Discover more about it in this brilliant timeline!

AD 1821
William Bucknell and other pioneers first travel west on the Sante Fe trail.

AD 1848
Gold is discovered at Sutter's Mill, California, sparking a gold rush.

AD 1860
The Pony Express is founded, delivering mail across America.

AD 1843
Thousands head west in the Great Migration.

AD 1852
The Wells Fargo company is set up to provide stagecoach services.

AD 1874
Gold is discovered in the Black Hills of Dakota.

AD 1869
The Transcontinental Railroad is finished.

AD 1866
The Long Drive: Cowboys drive cattle from Texas to the northern states of America.

AD 1870
Buffalo hunters move on to the plains.

AD 1881
Wyatt Earp takes part in the gun battle at the O.K. Corral in Tombstone, Arizona.

TIME HUNTERS TIMELINE

Tom and Zuma never know where in history they'll travel to next!
Check out in what order their adventures actually happen.

10,000 BC–3000 BC
The Stone Age.

AD 1427–AD 1521
The Aztec Empire

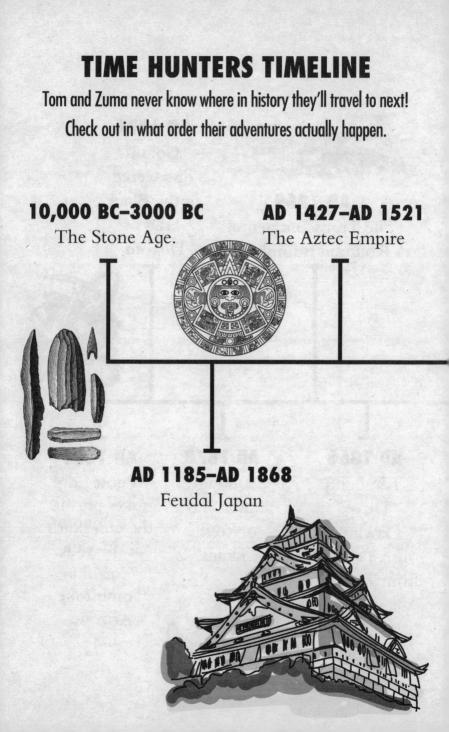

AD 1185–AD 1868
Feudal Japan

AD 1775–AD 1900
Era of the 'Wild West' in America

AD 1492–AD 607
First contact between Native American tribes and European settlers in America

AD 1850–AD 1880
Bushranger outlaws become famous in Australia

FANTASTIC FACTS

Impress your friends with these facts about the Wild West.

➤ Horses were so important that stealing one was considered a hanging offence! *That's not the way to get a-head in life...*

➤ Whenever there was a gunfight, this would usually take place in the middle of town at High Noon. *Number one on the 'Places to Avoid' list...*

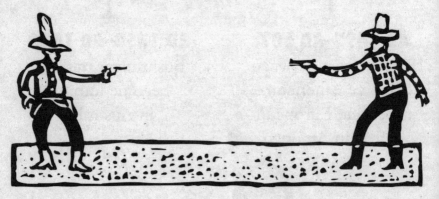

The infamous cowboy Wild Bill Hickok was first known as 'Duck Bill' because of his huge nose! *That's just quackers!*

 After eating beans, some cowboys were said to have called them 'Deceitful beans' because they 'talked behind your back'! *Parp!*

 Cowboys were among the first people to wear denim jeans. They were invented to be hard-wearing work trousers. *Genius jeans!*

WHO IS THE MIGHTIEST?

Collect the Gaming Cards and play!

Battle with a friend to find out which historical hero is the mightiest of them all!

Players: 2
Number of Cards: 4+ each

 Players start with an equal number of cards. Decide which player goes first.

 Player 1: choose a category from your first card (Brain Power, Fear Factor, Bravery or Weapon), and read out the score.

 Player 2: read out the stat from the same category on your first card.

➜ The player with the highest score wins the round, takes their opponent's card and puts it at the back of their own pack.

➜ The winning player then chooses a category from the next card and play continues.

➜ The game continues until one player has won all the cards. The last card played wins the title 'Mightiest hero of them all!'

COWBOYS
WYATT EARP

Brain Power	
Fear Factor	300
Bravery	285
Weapon: Bullwhip	320
	330
TOTAL	1235

For more fantastic games go to:
www.time-hunters.com

BATTLE THE MIGHTIEST!

Collect a new set of mighty warriors — free in every
Time Hunters book! Have you got them all?

COWBOYS

- [ ] Wyatt Earp
- [ ] Wild Bill Hickok
- [ ] Buffalo Bill
- [ ] Billy the Kid

SAMURAIS

- [ ] Lord Kenshin
- [ ] Honda Tadakatsu
- [ ] Lord Shingen
- [ ] Hattori Hanzo

OUTBACK OUTLAWS

- [ ] Ben Hall
- [ ] Captain Thunderbolt
- [ ] Frank Gardiner
- [ ] Ned Kelly

STONE AGE MEN

- [ ] Gam
- [ ] Col
- [ ] Orm
- [ ] Pag

BRAVES

- [ ] Shabash
- [ ] Crazy Horse
- [ ] Geronimo
- [ ] Sitting Bull

AZTECS

- [ ] Ahuizotl
- [ ] Zuma
- [ ] Tlaloc
- [ ] Moctezuma II

MORE MIGHTY WARRIORS!

Don't forget to collect these warriors from Tom's
first adventure!

GLADIATORS

- [ ] Hilarus
- [ ] Spartacus
- [ ] Flamma
- [ ] Emperor Commodus

KNIGHTS

- [ ] King Arthur
- [ ] Galahad
- [ ] Lancelot
- [ ] Gawain

VIKINGS

- [ ] Erik the Red
- [ ] Harald Bluetooth
- [ ] Ivar the Boneless
- [ ] Canute the Great

GREEKS

- ☐ Hector
- ☐ Ajax
- ☐ Achilles
- ☐ Odysseus

PIRATES

- ☐ Blackbeard
- ☐ Captain Kidd
- ☐ Henry Morgan
- ☐ Calico Jack

EGYPTIANS

- ☐ Anubis
- ☐ King Tut
- ☐ Isis
- ☐ Tom

Who were the Samurai?

What weapons did they fight with?

And how did you become a ninja?

Join Tom and Zuma on another action-packed
Time Hunters adventure!

Tom's eyes followed Zuma's pointing finger.
She had spotted a tall teenage boy sprinting
down a hill as if his life depended on it.

A few seconds later, Tom saw why.

The noise wasn't thunder — it was the

hooves of galloping horses. A group of
horsemen charged over the hill. Their leader
saw the running boy and pointed, screaming
at the men behind. He urged his sweating
horse to go faster. Looking over his shoulder,

the boy yelled in fright. The horsemen were
gaining on him. He put on a fresh spurt of
speed, heading straight for Tom and Zuma.

As the horsemen drew nearer, Tom
recognised their armour from an exhibit in

his dad's museum. It belonged to medieval Japanese warriors called samurai. Each warrior wore an iron breastplate, and skirts of overlapping leather protected their legs. Their helmets were decorated with what looked like alien antennae. Strapped to the samurai's backs were curved swords called katana. In the safety of the museum, Tom had thought the katana looked really cool. Up close they looked like deadly weapons.

"They're samurai warriors!" he called out to Zuma.

"They're big bullies, that's what they are!" she shouted back.

The boy was only a few metres from Tom and Zuma when he stumbled, twisting his ankle. He fell to the ground with a cry of pain.

Before Tom could blink, Zuma had run

over to his side. "Can you get up?" she asked. "Here… lean on me."

"Lean on me too," added Tom, running over to join them. Whatever magic Tlaloc used to transport them across time also made it possible for Tom and Zuma to communicate with everyone they met.

"Don't worry about me," the boy panted, staggering to his feet. "Get out of here before they catch you as well!"

"Tom!" shouted Zuma.

When Tom looked up, his face went white with fear. A wave of samurai horsemen was crashing down on them!

*

Tom's heart thumped like a drum. There was nowhere to hide. The tiny part of his brain that wasn't terrified told him it was useless to run. There was no way to escape the galloping horses. The three of them, and Chilli, would be trampled beneath the flying hooves.

He closed his eyes. Then a voice shouted, "Halt!"

Tom opened his eyes, amazed he was still alive. The samurai had pulled up their horses at the last second, and were now fanning out round Tom, Zuma and the boy. Within seconds, they were surrounded.

The same voice that had given the command spoke again. "Who are you?" it said, in a sneering tone.

Tom looked up. The samurai leader was glaring down at him from the back of his snorting black stallion. Beneath all the heavy armour, Tom could see he was a young man – barely older than the boy he had been chasing. His face was proud, his

eyes cruel and arrogant.

"We're travellers," Tom said quickly.

At his feet, Chilli growled. "Good doggie. Brave doggie," whispered Zuma, trying to calm down her pet.

"Well, travellers, I am Goro, the son of an important nobleman. You may bow."

Zuma snorted loudly. "I don't think so," she said. "I don't bow to anyone."

Goro's eyes blazed with anger. "You try to help Oda, the salt thief, and then you refuse to bow?" he barked. "Do you wish to share his punishment?"

"Salt thief?" giggled Zuma. "He stole some salt? Is that all?"

"Be silent, girl!" Goro commanded.

Zuma ignored him. "What a mighty warrior you are," she taunted. "Leading your men in a brave quest to capture a salt thief."

Goro's face had turned purple with rage. Tom elbowed Zuma. "Have you seen their swords?" he whispered. "Maybe you shouldn't—"

"Enough!" screamed Goro. "Perhaps watching me thrash Oda until he is black and blue will silence you." He held up a thick bamboo cane and the sunlight flashed on a silver ring he wore on his finger.

"Don't you dare," snapped Zuma. She stamped her foot. "I used to be a slave, so I know what it's like to be unfairly punished. If you want to thrash him, you'll have to get past me first."

"And me," Tom said, stepping in front of Oda.

Surprised, Goro lowered the cane. A sly grin crept across his face. "No," he said finally. "A thrashing would be too kind a punishment. The Dragon himself will punish you for your insolence."

Oda turned pale. Tom wanted to tell him not to worry and that there were no such things as dragons, but he decided to keep quiet. Goro was angry enough already. Whatever the samurai had meant, Tom knew that they had to escape. The riddle had mentioned a tiger, but said nothing about dragons. The last thing he wanted was to become a prisoner of the samurai.

It seemed Zuma had been thinking the same thing. "Look!" she cried out, pointing behind Goro. "Salt thief! And he's getting away!"

Goro grunted with surprise, and turned round in his saddle.

"Run!" Zuma hissed at Tom.

They both darted off in different
directions, trying to find a gap in the ring
of horsemen. Tom managed to take two
steps before he felt the sharp tip of a sword
pressing into his chest. He stopped in his

tracks. The samurai holding the sword smirked at him triumphantly. Looking across at Zuma, Tom saw that she had met the same fate. They were trapped.

THE HUNT CONTINUES...

Travel through time with Tom and Zuma as they battle the mightiest warriors of the past. Will they find all six coins and win Zuma's freedom? Find out in:

Got it! ☐

Got it! ☐

Got it! ☐

Got it!

☐

Got it!

☐

Got it!

☐

Tick off the books as you collect them!

DISCOVER A NEW
TIME HUNTERS QUEST!

Tom's first adventure was with an Ancient Egyptian mummy
called Isis. Can Tom and Isis track down the six hidden
amulets scattered through history? Find out in:

Got it! ☐

Got it! ☐

Got it! ☐

Got it! ☐

Got it! ☐

Got it! ☐

Tick off the books as you collect them!

Go to:

www.time-hunters.com

Travel through time and join the hunt for the mightiest heroes and villains of history to win **brilliant prizes!**

For more adventures, awesome card games, competitions and thrilling news, scan this QR code*: